To Champions everywhere
especially the Angels of my Heart

Katelin

Blake

Ashton

Arron

Tavery

Austin

Mark

Jenna

Trace

Shelby

Ty

Samuel

Cache

Stefan

Tiffany

Mercedes

Grapic Design by: Mark Paterson
Technical Design by: Marco A. SantaMaría

Published by NORTH STAR PUBLICATIONS,
10199 S.W.201 Terrace, Miami, Florida 33189

Printed in the U.S.A.

ISBN: 1-930458-01-0

CELEBRATE THE FIRE WITHIN

Written by Kathy Larsen

Illustrated by C.B. Decker

Do I have a spark,

A FIRE
WITHIN?

YES!

And it says
to me,
try, try
again.

I look up to
the stars and

I'll dare
to dream,

I WILL reach
my goal

with my own
special team.

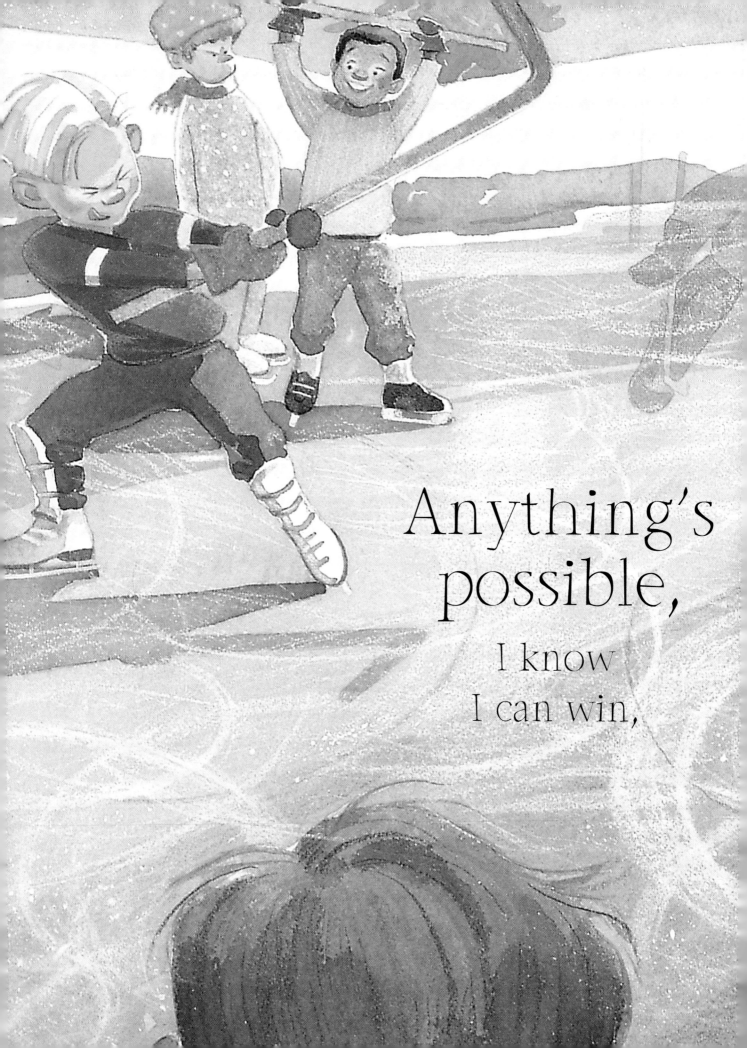

Anything's
possible,

I know
I can win,

My struggles
will fire my will to
begin.

At the top of
the peak,

I'm ready
to START.

This race of a
lifetime will
set me
apart.

Come and watch me fly, as I
REACH for the sky,
I'll give it my all,
every time that I try.

Faster and faster
with the wind
in my face,

There's no
better feeling,
I'll win any race.

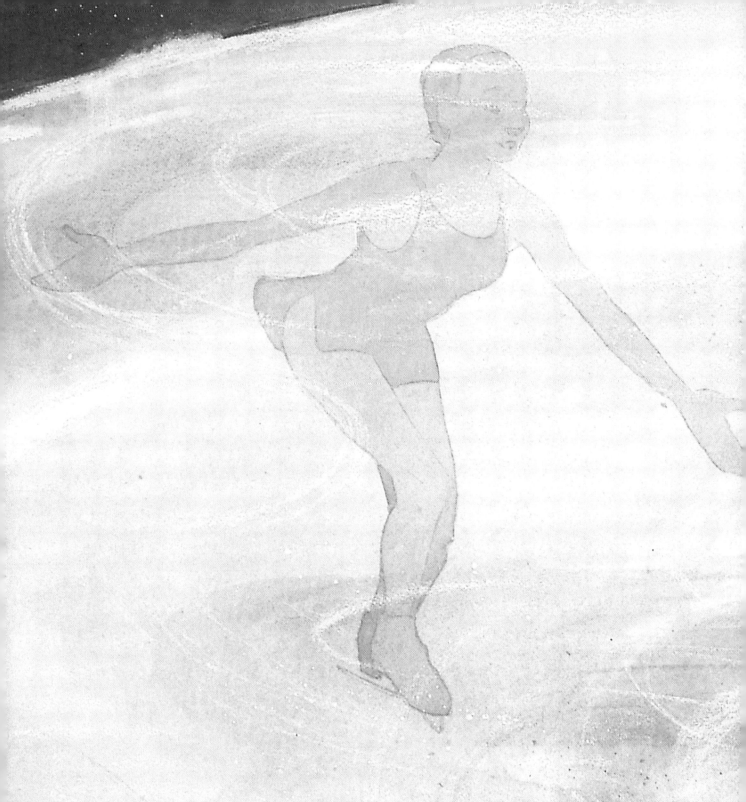

HOPE and hard work
will help carve out my story,

And one day
I'll reach for
Olympic
glory.

The WORK and the struggles,
I'll Cheerfully hide,

As I take to the ice and
gracefully glide.

I know a medal has
                untold measure,
But Olympic SPIRIT
is what I treasure.

The fire inside will bring us together,

And Olympic
memories will
last forever.

So come and celebrate
THE FIRE WITHIN,
Feel it, and share it,
and let it begin.

For The Reader

Did you know there is a champion inside of you?

There is. There really is.

We can find champions all around us if we really look. A champion is someone who does battle for the right or honor of someone else.

We call the Olympic athletes champions because they gather from around the world at the Olympic Games to give their all for their country and their team.

But Mom's and Dad's can be champions too, because they sacrifice their time and they work hard to make sure we are safe and happy.

Our teachers can be our champions as they teach us to learn and to be excited about all the wonderful things around us.

And what about you? Are you a champion? You can be. Yes you can. You can bring joy and inspiration as a son or a daughter, a brother or a sister, a friend or a neighbor. You can be a champion to those around you.

So whether you want to be an athlete or a teacher, a writer or a doctor, a carpenter or a lawyer, a Mom or a Dad, a president or a policeman; you can be a champion in anything you choose. It's already inside you to be the best you can be. All you have to do is fan the spark into a flame, work hard, and *Celebrate The Fire Within!*

By Patrick St. Clair for Kathy Larsen